A Battleaxe and a Metal Arm 10:

False Stars and Writing Night

Samuel Fleming

Thank you to my Beta Readers

and to my First Reader,

Mel.

iv

Contents

"To almost all the civilized
races, death is not the end.
I do not know whether it was
true elsewhere, but it is true
here."
—forgotten

Previously…

Helesys and Taunauk stepped into the realm of the Cogheart and found themselves face to face with their ally, Shawn. It seemed that the pair and the rogue were bound together by whatever loose threads of fate may be. They regaled Shawn about their journey through the caverns of Shéslang, and Shawn told them of his journey through the lost jungle filled with vicious lizards.

Shawn revealed that the Voice on the beach of Meridian said he was neither human nor elf—that his heritage was a mystery.

Helesys and Taunauk revealed their new memories as well: Her memory of joining the elven legion and shearing her hair short to do so. Taunauk revealed his memory of exile, confounded by his axe—a family heirloom that he was allowed to keep. Despite the mysteries, the group revelled in their company.

And in spite of their separation, with Helesys's power over the seams, the group was hopeful that they could stick together from then on.

The group struck out through the hallway, to a wide wasteland of black rock, dark skies and thunder storms. Helesys guided them with faint direction to a lone automaton—a creature of metal and mind.

Porthmeus was its name, and the solitary Cogheart led them to an underground entrance. There it revealed the presence of the realm's ruler, One-Mind, a Cogheart intelligence of staggering scope and size. Porthmeus opened the door to One-Mind's massive underground bunker, relaying that One-Mind would speak to them, but also warning them that each realm would bring danger—other automatons that acted on directions and did not think as Porthmeus did.

In the First Layer, the heroes had no choice but to outrun a guardian swarm of crawling and flying automatons. Helesys was able to channel both her Ring of Winter and the Gar of Shéslang into a massive wall of ice to block the swarm for a time as the heroes fled deeper and deeper into the underground bunker.

In the Second Layer, they rested at an underground lake, something that Helesys connected to the heat shedding technology that Porthmeus spoke of—she understood because she felt that elves used similar technology. Shawn took the moment to recall his memory of living with a human family and working in a smoke-filled factory.

Next, they came face to face with hunter-killers, specially made automatons that patrolled the inner layers and protected One-Mind. There was little room to fight in the narrow tunnels, and when the heroes found themselves beset on both sides and trapped, Helesys used her powers to bolster the strength and speed of her allies. Both Taunauk and Shawn were each able to defeat a hunter-killer, though they reacted differently afterward. Taunauk was hesitant to appreciate the help, because Helesys had touched his Rage. Meanwhile, Shawn was overjoyed at having more connection to his 'wind-like' powers.

Further in the Second Layer, they came upon a recycling cavern filled with great piles of decomposing scrap metal. There they ran into the hunter-killer abomination, Dissimul. Though the giant, twisted automaton could speak, it couldn't be reasoned with. In the end, it took the might of all three heroes—Helesys using her spear and wand-arm to bolster her strength and martial prowess, Shawn using his wind-speed, and Taunauk channeling fully manifested Endroggen spirits. In the end, they were forced to flee and came to the massive lake that marked the Third Layer.

There they heard the voice of One-Mind, which beckoned them onto a white platform that took them beneath the lake's surface. At the bottom of the lake, they reached the entrance to the Core, but One-Mind revealed that before they could enter, they had to deal with Dissimul—the rogue hunter-killer—who had tracked them to the bottom of the lake.

The resulting battle was hard-fought, but in the most desperate moments, Helesys was able to grasp and hold Dissimul with her magic. In the mind-space, she saw the abomination for what it truly was: A tiny, emerging personality. A copy. Something that One-Mind could not allow to exist. One-Mind un-made Dissimul, before beckoning the heroes into the Core to speak with it.

In the Core, the heroes found themselves in a small grove amidst a towering forest. One-Mind was a small metallic section within a giant swirl of rock. One-Mind revealed its origin in the Druid forest, that other mages had come and used magic to seal a copy of One-Mind in the mirror—that the One-Mind the heroes were speaking to was the copy.

That every so often, other copies emerge, like Dissimul, and must be culled.

Rather than escape or confrontation with the Wolf-King, One-Mind sought escape into another realm, one that it made and would control—just like the wizard Amadeus sought with his jade egg.

One-Mind repaired Helesys's wand-arm and revealed that such an injury was caused before she was trapped in the dungeon. The repair was a boon that would better allow them to walk between realms.

Such a power would enable them to find the Godpeak and the Machine of Antrikaumora. But it would also leave them vulnerable to the Wolf-King and to other nefarious creatures that lurked in the dungeon.

In the end, Helesys opened the seams, attempting to go to the Godpeak… But found themselves off course, affected by some nefarious, alien creature.

~ ~ ~

The Twisted Halls

The heroes stood apprehensively in the unfamiliar hall. Instead of the starting room, the wide hall stretched out into the distance. The walls were twisted and warped, the familiar sconces hung in lopsided angles off the wall. Above them, the bricks coalesced into stalactites, adding to the illusion that the room was melting.

The seam closed behind them, revealing a blank wall—one that seemed unmarred by whatever magic lingered there.

"Wait," Shawn said apprehensively. "What do you mean this isn't the Wolf-King's doing? Didn't One-Mind just give us a speech about Him tracking us if we dallied too long in the ether?"

Helesys was only half listening. She was reaching out with her wand-arm, searching for more clues about what they were dealing with. Whatever had brought them there was watching them.

Something even stranger than One-Mind, the glassmen, or any other gods they had come across. Something alien and powerful.

Taunauk stood beside her, already with Everfall shield and axe in hand. He eyed the twisted hall with the same weariness, no doubt already intuiting similar danger.

"It's something else," Helesys said, avoiding the reflex to whisper—it wouldn't help. Whatever the being was, it could hear them. "And it's scrying on us."

The rogue shivered, then quickly unsheathed twin daggers.

"Do you feel it now?" Helesys asked.

"No," Shawn replied. "The thought of it just gives me the willies."

The spellweaver sighed. "Come on, then. Let's not keep our host waiting."

"Can't we turn back?" Shawn asked. "Try a different seam?"

Even Taunauk looked at her, as if contemplating the same thing. Helesys kept a straight face, for the thought of pushing forward filled her with a dread that she didn't want to admit. Even though most deaths were merely an inconvenience in the dungeon, dying was still unpleasant. Besides, Helesys imagined that the realm had lingering deaths waiting for them.

Instead, she reached toward the seams again, opening herself to the tenuous magic that ran between realms. To the smells or feeling that marked a new destination… To any hint of a realm...

She found nothing.

And in the quiet corners of the hall, the faintest laughter bubbled through the cracks and warped crevices. Wet, hissing laughter.

Even Taunauk and Shawn heard it and felt it: The barbarian tensed and looked around, while the rogue shivered again.

"Alright," the rogue seethed. "Whoever's walking over my grave should kindly stop!"

"It won't let us leave," Helesys said, stepping forward, knowing that her allies couldn't understand the alien sounds. She kindled power in her wand-arm, while the magic spear hummed with anticipation in her other hand.

In spite of the exertion in the realm of the Cogheart, Helesys felt restored—powerful.

Shawn turned meekly. "Well, we could…" The rogue drew a finger across his throat. "Like to see the bastard stop us from doing that."

Helesys took his meaning, but Taunauk caught her eye, and she could tell that the barbarian was thinking the same as she. The weaver said, "We'll be split up again."

Shawn said jokingly, "That might be preferable to whatever lingering death or weird *stercus* is ahead of us. Even when we're split up, we do seem to find our way back together." There was a hint of reservation in his levity—one of a man who didn't really want to wander alone again.

The barbarian was still eyeing the walls hesitantly, but said, "Or you might run into a lingering death on your own."

The rogue crossed his arms. "Death for all or death for none, is that it?"

Helesys smirked, "Something like that."

"That's sweet," he replied with a dash of sarcasm.

"Alright, let's get on with it," Helesys said. "We have more pressing concerns."

Taunauk growled beside her, "Agreed."

~

The trio paced carefully down the hall, their eyes flitting from wall, to ceiling, to floor, endless stretch in front of them and growing stretch behind them—unsure of where their ominous host might strike from.

Hours drug on.

The twisted hall continued, the bricks and the lines rippling even more until Helesys felt like they were walking over a frozen stream. The floor itself became uneven, like the cable-lined floors of One-Mind's bunker. Meanwhile, the walls to either side were marred with intermittent cracks every thirteen paces, each a vertical oval shape and mirrored perfectly on both sides. The cracks had been imperceptible at first, but each subsequent opening in the brick grew both larger and deeper.

"What do you make of those?" Shawn asked, pointing his white dagger at one of the cracks.

Every few passes, Helesys would run her wand-arm over the cracks to sense if magic was present.

"So far, there's no magic," she replied.

Taunauk grunted. "They are too regular to be anything mundane."

Shawn replied, "What if they *are* harmless, and the creepy dungeon master—realm master—is just toying with us?"

Frustration oozed from the barbarian. Taunauk said, "This whole hallway is likely a trap. One meant to tire our legs, weather our resolve, and lull us to complacency. Like chasing prey to wear it down before butchering it."

Shawn mumbled, "Don't give breath to fate, big guy."

Taunauk snorted, but said nothing more. Meanwhile, Helesys pondered both their statements, and found disconcerting truth in both of them.

Helesys kindled more power in her gauntlet, concentrating on detecting any magic at all—dangerous or otherwise. All she felt was the vague pull of direction from down the hall.

And the ever present scrying gaze of whatever presence lorded over the realm… Just watching. Just waiting.

The elf grit her teeth. She understood Taunauk's frustration. Here they were with all their strength, all their potential, forced to creep about because they couldn't see traps *where they knew traps should be!*

~

Hours dragged on as the heroes walked.

The hallway continued to change. The brick was completely gone, morphed into a sleek dark purple stone, the surface of which was pitted and glistened in the ambient light. Planar surfaces of the hallway shifted, taking on a strange, animalistic appearance—ripple patterns predominated, reminding Helesys of the ribs of an animal. Knobby growths jutted out from the walls as well, some nearly the length of her arm.

The appearance of torches had become more and more intermittent until they disappeared completely; this coincided with the rise in the oval cracks in the wall. These had grown until they were some four feet tall and nearly two feet wide. Liquid fire swirled in the ovals now, neither hot nor magical; these gave light to the hallway in the absence of torches.

Helesys had checked and double checked the glowing ovals for magic, but found none. This was all the more disconcerting because each glowing oval they passed reminded Helesys of a cat's eye. She imagined the unseen creatures of the realm watching the heroes as they passed, leering at them from being the fiery mirrors.

"Still nothing?" Shawn asked. The rogue had taken to tossing a dagger in the air every few steps and catching it. He did this whilst concentrating on searching the room.

"Still nothing," Helesys replied. She tried to mask her irritation—to the rogue's credit, he'd only asked that question a handful of times since they'd started walking, and it felt like they'd been walking all damn day.

Taunauk had been silent for most of the walk. Frustration seemed to fuel him. She imagined the ridiculousness of the long hallway was stoking his rage, keeping it kindled instead of burning like a bonfire.

Still, the trek was wearing on them. Helesys felt it and she saw as much in her comrades. Their faces were hard set, their steps less measured. Even as Helesys kindled her power, she felt her concentration waning—steps and time seeming to blur.

If the hallway was truly meant to test their resiliency and their resolve, then it was working.

"We should rest," Helesys said. No one offered any rebuttal.

The three stopped in the dappled shadows between the fiery openings. Just to be sure, Helesys walked one stop further and checked all four surrounding ovals for lingering magic. She found nothing—the pools of fire peered back absently.

Shawn was already slumped against the wall and digging for food in his pack. Taunauk sat cross-legged, leaving a space in the middle for Helesys. She smiled wearily and sat between them. Then both the weaver and barbarian joined Shawn in eating jerky, nuts, and dried berries.

Helesys relished the nourishment, lingering on each bite of the tiny orange fruits. So often realms passed with urgency that they had taken little time to rest. And then each had reserves of magic or inherent resilience, and it was no wonder Helesys had only eaten a handful of times in their journeys. It was for the best, too, because they had already eaten one day's worth of their rations since they perished last.

She relished the company, quiet as it was for a time. The stillness and the silence too, though these Helesys imagined she only enjoyed because they had come so infrequently. There was a part of her that longed for battle, for hardship—even as she enjoyed the quiet. She was two halves of at odds with one another.

"Some hallway," Shawn mumbled sarcastically, breaking the silence. "Really like what you've done with the place—it doesn't even speak our tongue, does it?"

Helesys shrugged. "It hasn't *said* anything yet. It's just watching." She felt the scrying presence, even then.

"I feel like you always do the talking," he added, then leaned forward to talk to Taunauk. "Any insights, oh wise one?"

Taunauk had already finished eating and was staring straight ahead, eyes half-closed. Breathing deep and steady.

Shawn continued, "If you're tired, big guy, I can take first watch."

"No," Taunauk mumbled. "I'm listening."

Silence lingered between them before Taunauk spoke again. Weaver and rogue looked down the long hallways, wondering if Taunauk was sensing something that they did not.

Taunauk sighed in frustration and opened his eyes fully. "It is nothing. I will take first watch."

Helesys searched her comrade's eyes and found him unsettled and silent. But she did not pry, for she trusted the outlander's judgment. "Wake me when you're ready," she said. Taunauk nodded.

Shawn slumped down to the ground, head propped on one of the weird curves of the hall. He pulled his hood over his eyes. "Wake me after," he muttered. His breathing slowed a moment later, and it seemed like the rogue had already drifted off to sleep before she found a comfortable position.

Even with Taunauk keeping watch, Helesys knew sleep would be fleeting. Not with the ever-present scrying eyes watching them.

~

In spite of the leering, alien presence, Helesys managed some sleep. Quick and dreamless.

She woke to the gentle nudge. Taunauk sat beside her, Everfall beside him and battleaxe sitting across his lap.

Helesys rubbed the sleep from her eyes, pushed herself up to a sitting position, and leaned against the curved wall. "Did you notice anything? Anything at all?"

Taunauk glanced from one end of the hallway to another. "Absolutely nothing," he said quickly and with frustration. "Do you still feel the creature scrying on us?"

She nodded. "Perhaps it is more content with waiting than we are. Get some sleep, Taunauk."

The barbarian grumbled. "A foe more patient than an elf does not bode well." He relaxed, shield and back resting against the stone, and let his head hang forward.

Helesys smirked, both at his quip and at the fact that he was content to sleep sitting up.

Meanwhile, Helesys alternated looking down the halls and focusing on her magic awareness in hopes that she might gleam something—anything—from the creature's scrying.

Her watch dragged on, quietly and uneventfully—

Until she felt flickers of recognition in her wand-arm.

Though she couldn't see the creature, she felt it. The mind that had been utterly incomprehensible began to take form as if Helesys was looking through clouded glass. A silhouette that was Terran—limbs, torso, and head—but belied... *something else.*

Helesys thought back to her first impression—that the creature was stranger even than One-Mind. Stranger than a construct that was neither Terran nor alive. But at least One-Mind had spoken their tongue, even had familiar wants and desires. It used magic, even if it was too advanced for her to replicate.

This creature felt like staring at an insect, a mollusk, or a moss growing on a stone. Its scrying was not magic... it was through some other means. Even the fishmen and the faeries, who were so strange that Helesys couldn't translate their tongues, did not strike her so differently.

But in that moment of seeing the ethereal silhouette of the creature, she felt that they had two things in common: The need to survive, and the need to procreate.

The creeping nightmare that had been stalking them was now given form. And form was something that Helesys could fight. In that, she took solace.

Taps sounded to her right—like water dripping.

Helesys turned and saw a creature coming through the fiery mirror. Long and slender, like a spider's leg. It was a deep purple and knobbed at the end. Another leg slipped through without making a sound, save for gentle taps as the knobby toes touched the ground.

The weaver stood quietly, tapping the rogue and the barbarian as she did. She kindled power in her wand and held a finger to her mouth.

Both Taunauk and Shawn roused with a startle, but stayed quiet as the creature stepped through the portal.

A dozen more legs stepped through the portal, and then the whole of it was through. The creature stood as tall as Helesys, a bulbous head sitting atop the slender, folded legs. The head was criss-crossed with ripples and folds that reminded Helesys of the very hallway that they stood in.

The creature had no eyes nor ears, or any other discernible facial features, nor had it turned at all, but Helesys was certain that it *saw* them.

It walked to the center of the hallway, its body suspended like a marionette. Then pinpricks of orange appeared around its head. Growing.

Helesys felt the telltale hum of warning from her wand-arm. There wasn't any magic, but the weaver was sure that the creature meant to use some kind of power.

The pinpricks of orange grew, becoming fiery ovals on its skin. As they grew, so did the hum of warning from her gauntlet.

Helesys raised her hand and purple lightning crawled over the metal. Then let power fly.

The bulbous head of the creature burst and splattered green across the twisted walls. The legs fell twisted to the floor.

Beside her, Shawn whispered, "I thought you said there wasn't any magic in those things."

"There wasn't," she replied. "This *isn't magic*. This is something—"

Another set of spider-like legs stretched through the portal. And another set from the portal across from it.

Taunauk growled. Behind them, the same scene was playing out—four of the same creatures surrounded them, dots of orange growing on their skin.

The barbarian leapt with a silent fury and crashed, axe-first, upon the two monsters. Shawn turned and dashed for those on Helesys's side, moving as fast as a spectre. Shawn cut both down before Helesys had raised her wand-arm again.

"The score is two-two-one," Shawn said, pointing toward Helesys.

"To task!" the outlander growled.

Past Taunauk, a dozen more spider-like creatures stepped out of the fiery portals between their group, and then a dozen more stepped out in Helesys and Shawn's direction.

Helesys said to Shawn, "You and Taunauk take that side. I will cover this one." The rogue nodded and disappeared in a blink.

In front of her, a dozen creatures began to glow with fire, and Helesys met each with rapid bursts from her gauntlet. Blasts soared down the hall in silent screams, bursting each creature in turn.

Taunauk and Shawn tore through their creatures in flashes of axe and daggers.

Still, more creatures came through. This time, spider-like legs crawled out of every portal that Helesys could see. Even the furthest regions of her vision crawled with movement.

"Helesys!" the rogue called. "What now!"

Her eyes flitted uncertainly between her comrades, the halls, and the countless monstrosities creeping through. She searched for seams with which to escape and found none. The warning from her gauntlet grew to a high pitched ringing.

"Kill as many as you can!" she shouted.

The weaver turned to her side, grit her teeth, and churned power. The familiar warmth turned to a bonfire, the familiar hum grew to a rattle as she dredged her depths of power. Purple energy boiled along the surface of her arm.

She called on the Gar of Shéslang, and the spear answered. The metal that had once pierced a god howled with fervor, and the power compounded between the two artifacts until the metal of her arm roared.

Never before had she held such power, and Helesys found her body siphoning some of the energy intrinsically so as not to be killed in the blowback.

As the ranks of creatures glowed orange, Helesys leveled her hand and fired. Even with bolstered strength, she went deaf and blind from the blast. She flew back, rolling across the warped floor a dozen times.

When she finally stopped, Helesys lay slumped against the corner of the hall. Her body sparked with agony. The Gar of Shéslang was gone. Taunauk and Shawn were distant blurs.

And in the direction of her blast, more creatures were stepping through the portals. The hall began to grow bright.

"So much for that," Helesys muttered.

She kindled power again, this time turning it inward. Bolstering her strength, resilience, and her mental defenses. It was a gamble, but that was all she had left.

Bright orange light erupted in the hall. Helesys shut her eyes and shied away, but still she saw the light.

~ ~ ~

Trapped

Helesys came too, so groggy that it was a struggle merely to open her eyes. She was standing upright. Her entire body, save for her head, was wrapped in a cocoon. Her left ear throbbed and the neck beneath it felt wet and chilled, as if she'd been bleeding from it.

All around her, hundreds of others were trapped similarly. The room was circular, with concentric rings of prisoners. Helesys was in the middle, and she couldn't see Taunauk or Shawn. The rings descended to a branching walkway.

She struggled against the confines, but couldn't budge her arms or her legs. If she could just get free, then she could find Taunauk and Shawn.

Helesys kindled power in her wand-arm, meaning to bolster her strength, when she heard a quiet voice.

You're finally awake.

Helesys glanced either direction, but only saw unconscious Terrans. No one met her eyes.

A moment later, she realized that the voice was magical, speaking directly to her without the need for sound.

You don't remember me, but I know you, Helesys of Great House Byyra. Don't worry. I'm on your side, and I'm going to get you out of here.

The voice was right—Helesys didn't recognize it. It was neither male, nor female, nor Terran. Nor was it the Voice from the beach of Meridian. It had the same oiled, metallic voice that One-Mind and Porthmeus had spoken with. Yet, this one was new entirely.

Helesys concentrated her thoughts, and directed a question to the voice: *Who, or what, are you?*

I'm your wand—what else would I be?

Helesys's mouth hung open, speechless.

It was a strange concept… Yet not impossible. Somehow she knew that when magic coalesced into places or imbued into objects, that wondrous, unforeseen things could happen. Even the Gar of Shéslang felt like it longed for battle—if it could be phrased such a way.

Of all the questions swirling in Helesys's mind, the first uttered was: *You can talk?*

Every time you wander into a dangerous situation, I've been warning you. One-Mind repaired the connection between us, so now you can actually hear me.

Helesys shook her head. *Enough,* she thought. *I—we—need to get free.*

One step ahead of you. You were right that the creatures don't use magic; they are pinnacles of biology. They don't need magic or metal or fabric, and can think and make things happen. The attack those creatures used against you was a form of psionics—the power of thought.

Helesys turned her attention outward, searching for the scrying ALIEN. But she didn't sense it at all anymore. That was why its touch had felt so impossibly different from the magic of Zhug, Amadeus, and One-Mind. The bastard wasn't using magic at all!

The wand continued: *But they are creatures of flesh and bone, as is their architecture. The stasis pod you're trapped in is made from the same flesh as the creatures.*

Helesys grinned. *Which means I can affect it with my magic.*

Our magic, yes.

The weaver ignored the comment and focused on the pod she was trapped in. What she found was a sliver of hardened flesh, like the carapace of an insect, with little blood and less feeling. However faint, the pod belied more, and Helesys followed it like she was following the root of a tree.

All the pods in the room were connected, and Helesys felt that they were one small part of something much larger. A massive structure of bone, sinew, and shell… There were dozens of compartments. In these, she felt other vague signs of life: Prisoners, like herself, and creatures that interacted with the structure with their psionic abilities.

Slowly, Helesys realized that they were no longer within the walls of the dungeon. They were inside a gigantic living ship. A formidable, but impossibly simple creature; Helesys couldn't feel any other signs or emotions within it, save for the simplest notion of life. It was as if the structure had been grown and shaped into this one purpose, as a farmer worked a field.

Helesys followed the sinew and bone of the ship back to her pod, and bid it to open—in her mind, Helesys spoke the word: *Itith*. The pod slipped loose around her, like a flower blooming. Its leaves parted, allowing her to step free. The Gar of Shéslang fell from between the folds, and Helesys seized it before it struck the ground.

She touched the skin of her wounded ear and neck, and her fingers came back slick with blood and mucus, with threads of blue within it.

Never mind that, her wand said. *I've taken care of it. We need to find the others.*

Helesys spun around, searching the stillborn faces of those trapped. She found Taunauk two rows behind her. His stubble-covered head and face was frozen and the pod bulged around the width of his shoulders. She ran up the uneven walkway to his pod.

"Taunauk," she whispered, but the outlander didn't stir. Her gaze was drawn to his left ear—which had a similar blood and mucus mix pooling in the crevice.

Helesys reached up and rested her metal hand on his forehead. Then she reached out with her magic, searching for the barbarian she had come to know well.

How was I able to wake when they weren't? Helesys asked her wand.

We were joined with certain safeguards in mind. You'll find that gives us a few more tricks and surprises than the other mages—even more now that all our linkages were repaired.

The weaver grinned in satisfaction, then quickly went back to the task at hand.

It felt as if she were searching for her friend in the dark and without aid of flame or magic. She called to him, and Taunauk answered weakly, distantly. But each time, she grew closer to rousing him.

Moments later, instead of Taunauk's voice, uncountable voices answered instead—their voices overlayed and unintelligible. A cacophony.

In front of her, the barbarian's eyes opened and his skin glowed golden. His face twitched quickly between several expressions—surprise, smile, agony, and a grimace.

A breath later, the glow faded from his skin and a fleshy pulp oozed from his left ear—the same mix of blood, mucus and blue strands that Helesys had found on her.

In her mind, the weaver again spoke the word *itith*, and the pod leaves parted to free her comrade. Taunauk stepped forward, shaking the discomfort and nausea from his face. He, too, reached a hand to his ear.

"I think they put something inside us," Helesys whispered. "I was able to overcome it with my wand, and it looks like your ancestral power saved you."

"What of Shawn?" Taunauk asked, pulling the axe from his back.

Across the room came the sounds of another pod opening. Helesys turned and saw Shawn's wispy hair just above the pods. The rogue had freed himself and was walking toward them.

The weaver breathed a sigh of relief until he made it to the center of the walkway. The rogue seemed outlined in mist, as if his form were dissolving. His pupils glowed a faint green.

"Get behind me," Taunauk said. The barbarian stepped forward, glowing. And from his body stepped three more glowing warriors, each adorned in molten skin and fur, their swords dripping magic.

Helesys stepped back and compounded her magic. She would need to seize Shawn and do so quickly—

Shawn lunged forward with eyes that weren't his own, with such speed that Helesys couldn't discern his movements, nor the daggers he wielded. The clangs of weapons overlapped until they sounded like rain on a metal roof—until they sounded like a downpour. Taunauk and the golden warriors became a blur.

On the deck of the *Malorienta*, Helesys had used her magic to hold tens of sailors at once. Shawn was not one of them. He had proven to be immune to certain magics. Moments ago, she had so easily reached out into the darkness and found Taunauk, but even with amplified power, she struggled to hold Shawn—to even find him.

Helesys called upon the Gar of Shéslang, bolstering her power further—

She caught the faintest glimpse of Shawn in the ether. A man as light as the wind, with as much magic, mystery, and potential flowing through him as there was in her and in Taunauk.

The very same power that ran through him helped Shawn slip her mental grasp. She could not hold him.

But the weaver felt something else. This she grasped and tugged at. It was slick and evasive, but nothing compared to the rogue. She found the slithering, mucus covered creature and seized it.

"Restu sonmovo, larvo."

In front of her, Shawn fell limply into Taunauk's arms. The golden warriors smoldered and dissolved into smoke. Shawn's face was still pale. The rogue wasn't moving or breathing.

In mindspace, Helesys stared at the slug inside Shawn. The blue veined creature shivered at her gaze.

Dithiit, she whispered—*Get out.*

The pitiful thing did not argue. Helesys eased her holding spell enough and moments later, blood trickled from the rogue's left ear. Then the wriggling thing emerged and plopped to the ground.

It started to crawl away, but Helesys knelt and whispered, "*Siccum putredine.*" Deathly mist flowed from her metal fingers to the slug. It twitched, shriveled, and then died.

The weaver felt a pittance of psychic recoil from the spell. Such a small thing. But the weaver's annoyance was overshadowed by her questions.

Why did I do that? Helesys asked her wand. Until then, Helesys had thought the blight spell only worked on plants. ...She wasn't sure why she had tried it on a living, moving creature.

That was your own volition. Your own intuition, the wand replied. *I only ask for credit when it's due. The blight spell saps the water from plants. It seems that these creatures are heavily dependent on water.*

Helesys half-heard the wand's answer. She was too busy focused on how she couldn't tell the difference between the wand's motivations and her own. Before, she had at least some idea of where the wand ended and she began. Now she wasn't so sure. It dawned on her that she would spend from then on second guessing her own thoughts.

Coughing brought her back to the moment. Shawn's coughing.

The rogue was folded over on his hands and knees. Coughing. Breathing. Color coming back to his face.

Taunauk was staring at her curiously, one hand on their comrade's back, the other still clutching his axe. "Something on your mind?"

"Later," was all she replied. "We need to get out of here."

The circular room full of captured prisoners loomed around them.

Shawn finally stood, his face clammy with sweat. "That was decidedly *not* fun. Thanks for going easy on me, by the way," he said sarcastically to Taunauk.

The barbarian grinned. "I would've been gentler but you were trying to get to Helesys. And your knives are scary."

"Daggers," Shawn corrected. "Besides, everyone knows you go for the weaver first."

"That's a sound tactic. Glad to see you're still your usual witty self," Helesys said with a smirk. She closed her eyes and set to task

Taunauk turned his attention to the passageways off of their room. "Why aren't they coming?"

Helesys reached back to the living ship, searched it, but she found nothing more than the simple creature. She couldn't feel the touch of scrying or any other creatures connected to it.

She quickly explained the living ship to her comrades, then added, "I think releasing Shawn was a defensive reflex. They must assume we would hesitate in killing one of our own."

"Why leave us with weapons at all?" Shawn asked.

Helesys shrugged. "Likely for the same reason that the scrying one no longer watches us. Hubris. They have *psionic* abilities—different from magic. They didn't think we'd make it out. When we were in the hallway, I heard it *laughing* at us."

Shawn's eyes narrowed. "Well, I didn't like them much before, and I certainly don't like them any more now."

"What about the others?" Taunauk asked, his eyes flitting from pod to pod. Nearly all held a Terran—elf, human, fishman, and several others that Helesys had never seen before.

"We can't risk it," she whispered. "We might be overrun, or the other aliens might notice."

Both her comrades looked weary of the decision, but neither offered a counter.

"Aliens," Shawn mused. "Now that's a thought."

~

Shawn snuck three dozen paces ahead, while Helesys tapped into the living ship and directed him. Taunauk followed at her back, silent as a wolf.

Helesys asked her wand, *Still there?*

Yes, but it is easier to communicate direction and warning the old way—through feeling. Easier and faster. Do not worry, Helesys Byyra. I am with you, always.

The weaver felt truth and warmth in the wand's statement—and also that those two sentiments were two distinctly different things… Helesys resolved to ask her wand about it.

She turned her attention back to her mind's eye view of the ship. Not only could she sense the structure and layout, but she could sense the vague presence of other creatures on board—the sleeping, captured Terrans of the room behind them, a group of hungry, simple creatures up ahead, and another…

This last presence was the furthest away from them, yet the deepest mind that was tied to the ship. Helesys wagered that it was the scryer.

How am I sensing all this? Helesys asked her wand.

The creatures do not use magic themselves, but it seems they know enough about it. The ship's engines use bottled magic for propulsion, and these systems are tied into the ship with technology like that which binds us together.

Helesys's legs suddenly felt shaky and her legs weak. *What does that mean? How did my people come across this technology?*

Spells and technology have been invented by multiple races over the years. The elves and the druids discovered similar spells without contact. Now really isn't the time for it. For now, think of the ship's engines as a magic backdoor.

Shawn snuck to the corner of the next room and looked back to his comrades. Helesys motioned for him to continue in, then she and Taunauk followed.

In the next room, the walls and ceiling were lined with bones that arched up to the ceiling; the skin of the walls was pulled taught, giving the impression of standing in a gaunt rib cage. A large pool took up the center of the circular room. The water was dark orange, murky and rippled with movement. As the heroes regarded the pool, the water belched sickly sweet bubbles, somewhere between ripe and rotten fruit.

"What the *stercus*—" Shawn started to say.

Something slithered to the surface. Something slug-like with iridescent blue veins.

The rogue shivered and backed away. "I've had about enough of that."

Taunauk turned his attention to watching further down the halls. "Are you sure no one's coming?"

"I'm sure," Helesys replied, "but it doesn't hurt to keep a lookout." She looked a moment longer before realizing that she had seen another such creature before. "Taunauk, do you remember the underground? When we ran into the lizard and the hive?"

Taunauk peered again at the rippling pool and the lazy slugs. "Gods… Was the greatworm one of these things?"

"It's too uncanny a resemblance," she replied. "Maybe that one escaped from its host."

"Helesys!" Shawn whispered.

She whirled around to find Shawn standing in front of a glowing green oval.

"What did you do?" the weaver asked. "What's wrong?"

"Not a damn thing," Shawn replied, unmoving. "It was blank a moment ago. All I did was walk over here… Now I'm afraid to move."

The weaver held out her gauntlet to the portal. There was no magic—same as before, but this time she reached out through the ship.

"There must be something," she mumbled.

Indeed, she felt something distant, like a candle flickering at night across the horizon.

Helesys took a tentative step closer and felt the candle growing in her mindspace. With each step forward it grew until her metal hand was inches away and the flame was glaring bright green in her mind. Captivating.

"Helesys…" Taunauk muttered.

She touched it, and as she did, the ship fell away. Helesys saw a vision around her.

~ ~ ~

Another Life

In the vision, Helesys was in a murky, orange world, surrounded by blue veined slugs. She crawled, feeling her body
undulating across the bottom of the spawning pool.

The weaver was reliving a memory—a bottled memory. Yet
it was more than just sight and sound and smell and touch. In
the murky tank, she felt warmth and comfort—that these
other slugs were her brethren. But she also felt longing, that
this was not where she was meant to stay for long. That eventually she would wither and die in the spawning pool… That
the orange murk was the remnants of her brethren long passed
and recycled into nourishment for the newborns.

Helesys felt a hand wrap around her slithering body, and it
picked her up out of the tank. *This* was significant, perhaps the
most significant part of the creature's life. Being chosen.

Outside of the tank, the slug's vision was blurry. All Helesys
could see was a whirl of color, and then flesh—the spiral of an
ear, and then darkness as she climbed inside. Her body thinned
as she slithered through the passage. She ate through the delicate skin and thin bone that protected the brain. Then flattened

herself across the grooves of her mate's delicate, delicious brain.

The slug—Helesys—was only vaguely aware of her mate's screams, for they were silent, breathless, and quickly pushed aside. What had been a Terran, was pushed to the back of its own mind, and drowned in a sea of unconsciousness. Left to float in a void more desolate than the night sky.

Mere breaths later, Helesys saw through her mate's eyes and her ears. In time, there would be nothing left of the Terran. The slug would bond with its brain, grow tendrils through its face, down its spine and along its bone. Pink skin turned a mottled purple. Red blood turned to blue.

Soon there would be only Idnauthi. This one's name was *Sigun*.

And in the vision, Helesys saw the Idnauthi do this to other Terrans. Saw them wander the twisted hall, frightened and confused at the alien geometry. They were incapacitated by a trap that was generations in the making, then floated through the air like marionettes suspended by her psionics. Sigun plucked more slugs—larva—from the pool and placed the chosen inside worthy hosts.

Helesys saw Sigun mingling with other adults. The creatures spoke through psionics. They touched affectionately through the nerve-rich tendrils that draped from their faces like the thin blue arms of a squid. But these others would not stay, for the Idnauthi had a long journey ahead of them.

Last, the weaver saw their tentative goodbyes. The adults climbed into rows and rows of freezing tanks aboard the ship. These would slow their organs down so that they would fall into an ageless, dreamless sleep, for the stars were so very far away and they were going back home. She watched Sigun place adults into freezing tanks, even its elders. Sigun bid them fare-well.

Once again, Sigun had been chosen. And this time was the most significant of Sigun's life, by far. For now, it was responsible for the rest of its race. It would never enter the freezing tanks. It would pilot the ship through the vastness of space, giving its life so that the rest might live free again.

Not trapped in the *iihdii*—in the *dungeon*. They would escape to the stars.

Eventually, the spawning pool would be closed over. The larva would live for many years in the brine, eating each other, recycling each other, but no one knew if the larva would make it to the next star.

Helesys saw the history of them faintly: They were a distant, space-faring race, one of conquerors and parasites. They traveled the stars, seeking planets with intelligent life. A single ship might scout, then use psionic relays to communicate back to their homeworlds, seeking reinforcements to conquer and enslave the world. They cared not for water or gold or anything else, save life, for they could make none of their own.

Last, the weaver felt the idle musings of her Idnauthi. Thoughts it had not shared with any other, save for the memory mirror. It was chance when the larva was chosen from the spawning pool. Chance when it was chosen to keep watch over its brethren—that it should be awake during the long frozen sleep. It was chance when their ship crashed *here*. It would be chance if they ever escaped.

Again, Helesys felt the word, *iihdii*—the *dungeon*. This word caused the creature great distress, for even though it referred to the dungeon, the castle, and the endless prison, the word didn't mean dungeon… it was the Idnauthi word for where a host's mind went when a larva took over them. That prison in their own mind, the sea of unconsciousness more desolate than the night sky.

She didn't know what was worse: To be entrapped in such a place, never to escape, or to be born there and never see freedom.

Helesys shivered at the thought, just as Sigun did. But the weaver turned her attention from the memories of the creature and its race to that of the ship.

~

She searched the ship's legacy for any memories from beyond… Of all the souls they had met in the dungeon and along their journey, many came to remember their lives before the dungeon, but none remembered the moments of being trapped. Even One-Mind did not remember—it only remembered being terrified.

She found the last memory. Right before the ship was trapped.

As the ship, Helesys hurtled through space far faster than any Terran or sea-faring ship or bird. So fast, she could feel the stars turning around her, and even this was slow because they were so very far away.

They were soaring toward a new planet, toward a new world to conquer.

But instead a speck appeared in the center of the ship's vision. Unexpected and uncharted. They were flying so fast that neither the ship nor the crew had time to avoid it.

In those final moments, the speck grew large in the ship's memory, blossoming from a dot until it usurped the entire forward view. So fast, Helesys merely saw a blink.

A bulbous cloud, pulsing, writhing as if it were alive. The faces of the trapped and the damned struggled beneath the surface like blood boiling beneath the skin—screaming in muted agony as they suffered and died and were reborn. Over and over again.

And Helesys felt *fear*—so potent and primal that even the ship felt it, even the ship shuddered. Even through the dull senses and simple mind of the ship, Helesys felt the indescribable terror. She was reminded of the pulsing hunger of the Duoausongur, of the living, writhing city—its overwhelming, singular, desperate voice.

And the parasite was nothing compared to what Helesys saw.

Even the *iihdii*, being trapped and buried within her own mind, was nothing compared to this.

Helesys saw *the dungeon*—its true form, outside of the sprawling tunnels, infinite castle and grounds. In that moment, she saw—she felt—the true horror. Being maimed and killed over and over with no end or mercy. Trapped so deep that the gods couldn't find her or hear her, let alone save her. The most merciful end one could hope for was a lingering death—something akin to *iihdii*, or the parasite, or some other fate too unspeakable to contemplate—those were better than the bulbous *thing* that Helesys saw.

Now the weaver knew why no creature or god in the dungeon remembered those last moments before being trapped—those last moments before they looked upon *the dungeon* for the first and the last time.

Before they were swallowed by the barely comprehensible horror.

~ ~ ~

Revelations

"...I don't think—"

Taunauk's voice was distant, even as the vision fell away and the green oval and rib-like walls of the room appeared again. Helesys recoiled violently from the vision, spinning right into Taunauk and nearly knocking the barbarian off his feet.

Taunauk wrapped his arms around her, his eyes wide. "It's okay. Whatever happened, it's okay now."

Helesys stared at him blankly. Every time she blinked, she saw a shadow of the writhing cloud—the dungeon—and each time she shuddered.

"*Stercus*," Shawn whispered, clutching the Gar of Shéslang. He had caught it before it hit the ground. "Is she alright?"

Finally, the nightmare faded from the corners of her vision, and the weaver's breathing slowed. Helesys nodded and Taunauk released her.

She wearily took the spear from Shawn. "How long was I out?"

Taunauk shook his head. "You reached for the oval and then recoiled in fright."

"By Movernus, it felt like hours."

"What did you see?" he asked.

Helesys looked to the spawning pool. "I saw them, their race, and their history. And then *I saw it.*"

"You saw what?" Shawn asked, stepping closer.

Helesys took a steady breath. "They say that in time, we'll remember our lives from before we were trapped here. But no one—not Amadeus or One-Mind or anyone else—remembers what trapped them. But *I saw it.* I looked through the vacant eyes of the ship as they crashed into it."

"Into what?" Shawn's voice had grown frantic. Taunauk's eyes were wide.

"I saw the dungeon." A chill ran down Helesys's back as she recounted the vision. "It looked like a living cloud, like maggots writhing beneath skin… Gods, I wish I could unsee that."

Taunauk and Shawn glanced at each other, then eyed her wearily.

"You don't believe me?" she asked.

"It's not that," Shawn said quickly. "It's just… You didn't see your face. In all the horrible shit we've seen. I've never seen you scared—not like that."

Helesys just shook her head. She had no words. Nothing that could convey what she'd seen or what she'd felt—not truly.

Taunauk laid a heavy hand on her shoulder. "There are things mortals were not meant to see. The fact that you are still standing is a testament to your strength—"

Helesys's gauntlet hummed with warning just as steps and growls echoed from down the hall—back the way they came. From the room where they were bound.

It knows, her wand said. *Sigun knows you've escaped.*

Helesys turned to the rogue. "See what's around the next corner. Taunauk and I will hold them here." Shawn was gone a moment later.

The weaver turned to the outlander. "Don't kill them," she said. "I think there is another way."

Taunauk eyed her wearily, but didn't argue. He stood in front with Everfall and axe at the ready.

Then a horde rounded the corner of the hall. Dozens of Terrans ran toward them, eyes and faces blank, weapons in hand, blood staining the ears and necks of all.

Helesys kindled power, pulling from both her wand and from her spear. She grasped the spear with both hands, whispered "*Siccum putredine*," then slammed the butt of the spear to the ground with a resounding crack. Mist burst forth and rushed toward the horde, filling the hallway.

Still, the Terrans ran toward them.

It will take time, her wand said, and Helesys repeated the words aloud for Taunauk.

As the mist faded, Helesys instead turned energy to her body and to the Gar of Shéslang—careful not to dump too much power into her strikes.

She stood shoulder to shoulder with her comrade, battering each successive Terran with the blunt ends of her spear. Knocking weapons from hands, striking their torsos to stun them and push them back. Taunauk bashed with his shield and the flat end of his axe. He did this stoically and muted, silent as a jungle cat. It was one of the only times she could remember her comrade fighting silently and without rage.

The Terrans crashed impotently against them and fell back with equal vigor. So long had Helesys and Taunauk been fighting monsters and horrors, that mere Terrans did not move them.

Many of the Terrans looked no different than they might've before, save for pale faces and their absent eyes. But some were midway through their transformation into Idnauthi; their skin was growing purple and mottled. Their faces grew patchy beards made of thin dangling skin instead of hair and streaked with the blue veins of the larva infesting them.

Already, the normal-looking Terrans began to spasm in piles on the floor of the hallway. Blood and muck seeped from their ears as the larva inside died from Helesys's blight spell. But the others, those already midway through transformation, fought on. They rose after each blow and attacked with fervor. Their faces flushed red and green, and grew mad with anger or desperation as the blight spell took effect. Soon, they too fell and began to writhe on the ground.

The hallway was filled with twitching hosts. Dying larva limped out from many, fell to the floor, and were crushed by struggling neighbors.

Helesys watched spellbound as the scene grew still, as more and more of the Terrans were freed. More, but not all.

Those Terrans that had not begun to transform, rose and looked around wildly in confusion. To these, Helesys said in the common tongue, "Do not be afraid. We are your allies."

Those that were already in the midst of transformation lay still on the ground, blood trickling from their ears.

As the moment passed, and Helesys released power from her wand and her spear, she finally felt the recoil of the blight spell. It was a small thing to kill the larva—things had not become—but for those half transformed, she felt a stab of pity. Not just for those Terrans buried in the *iihdii*—in their own minds and lost—but also for the Idnauthi.

This gave Helesys pause. Why did she pity those dying Idnauthi? They had killed and enslaved countless Terrans. Their species had likely done so for hundreds or thousands of years. Immeasurable suffering. How could she feel pity for a species whose very existence revolved around enslaving the minds and bodies of others? Yet, she felt pity for them all the same.

Perhaps you feel for them because they are only doing what they must to survive, her wand said. *It's not merely that they don't know any different, but because they have no choice in the matter.*

They are monstrous to you, as surely as you are a soldier. How many times did you act without thought or without choice?

Helesys shot back, *It is not the same. I am choosing to be different.*

I am merely helping you parse your thoughts, her wand replied.

~

"Helesys," Taunauk growled.

She returned to the moment, to the half-dead, half-comatose mass of Terrans in the hall, and found the barbarian staring across the room.

The weaver followed his gaze across the spawning pool and the room, and saw an Idnauthi—Sigun—standing in the opposite hall, holding Shawn by the throat—the rogue hanging limp in its grasp.

It stood nearly eight feet tall on long, knobby limbs. A long, frilled robe draped from its back, the ends frilled like orange coral. Its skin was purple, smooth and hairless, save for its face. Dozens of tendrils hung from its chin like a stringy beard, each blazened with the blue veins of the parasite that had grown inside its skull, changing and warping its host until there was nothing left of the original body save for the vaguely Terran shape.

And it stared back at her, its milky gray eyes narrowing.

Behind her, the still-living Terrans roused and muttered wildly.

The tendrils of Sigun twitched, and Helesys heard a hoarse, dripping whisper in her head. *"Be still, carapaci!"*

Before the sentence was through, the Terrans were seized and pulled upright, hanging in the air on their toes like marionettes.

Helesys tried to raise her gauntlet, power rumbling within it, but found herself frozen—palm open and purple crackling around it, but pointing at the ground.

She gasped for air and found her chest moving as if nothing was the matter.

Beside her, Taunauk roared and charged at Sigun. The creature turned to him and as Taunauk charged he left golden warriors in his wake, each frozen mid-stride like afterimages. And as Taunauk hoisted his axe to slice through the Idnauthi, he froze mid-swing.

"You insolent creatures," Sigun said. It lowered its hand, and still Shawn hung in the air beside it. *"You've already forgotten your place."*

The rogue met Helesys's eyes from across the room, and she breathed a sigh of relief that he was still alive.

The Idnauthi strode past the frozen Taunauk, not even bothering to look at him or his glowing spirits. It walked so gracefully that it seemed to float across the room, and stopped to the left of Helesys. In front of the hallway of frozen Terrans.

As it approached, Helesys began to sense its power. The psychic power, its psionics, seemed to radiate off it like heat from a flame.

And Helesys recognized it.

She was reminded of the creeping, oppressive minds of the blue Terrans. The feeling of their breath upon her neck and whisper in her ear. Their power felt so eerily similar to the Idnauthi. Then she remembered her wand's insight from earlier: *Spells and technology have been invented by multiple races over the years.* Had the blue Terrans from the forgotten city developed similar power even though they were worlds apart? She thought too of the island creatures they had passed on the Malorienta, and how their magic had been similar, yet different—Shawn had been immune to that magic, but not this.

As unsettling and oppressive as the psychic power of the blue Terrans had been, Sigun's power was even greater—and it was alone!

Helesys thought of its scrying in the hallway, and even of its display of power now. Of it reaching across the room with such direction and efficiency. Stopping her motion without stopping her breathing.

And yet Helesys could feel and recognize its power.

Beside her, the Idnauthi loomed over the hallway, resonating power and menace.

Helesys steeled herself and spoke to the creature in its own alien tongue. *"Come here, Sigun."*

The creature's gray eyes widened in muted surprise. It glided over to her, and Helesys felt its power growing more potent with each step. Closer and closer until it was close enough to touch. Pungent and sour smelling, its tendrils rippling.

"How dare you look into my mind's eye," Sigun whispered. *"How dare you speak your master's tongue."*

Helesys ignored him and kept talking. She needed to understand its power, and she could only do that by keeping it close.

"I saw the dungeon," Helesys said. *"I know you want to go to the stars. We seek escape too."*

Sigun laughed quietly at her, its blue tendrils rippling in waves. *"You cannot even escape this ship."*

Helesys face wrinkled in annoyance that she could no longer contain. *"Are all your kind so arrogant?"*

"Only when speaking to carapaci."

While they spoke, Helesys studied and plotted.

She had been right—the Idnauthi's psionics were nearly identical to that of the blue Terrans. She hadn't been able to feel or understand them because Sigun was much more adept at hiding and wielding its power. The blue Terrans had been desperate and wielded their psychic power like a cudgel; Sigun wielded it like a surgeon.

Yet, Helesys also knew that the Sigun was hiding its true power—hiding that it was *far weaker* than it currently appeared.

Ahah, Helesys thought, biting her cheek to keep from smiling. She had a wand, a ring, and a staff bolstering her strength. *Sigun had a ship.*

She could feel the tenuous connection between Sigun and the living ship. A connection could be severed. Power could be countered.

Helesys peered sideways at Sigun. *"Let us go and I'll let you live. Test me and you will never see the stars."*

"Insolent weaver, you will never be free—"

She had heard enough. Helesys had cast off the creeping minds of the blue Terrans with a fury. With Sigun, she merely wriggled in his grasp, just enough to cast a spell.

"Restu sonmovo, vivamus navis." Helesys reached for the ship and found it easily. Such a colossal being, yet purposely made weak so that the Idnauthi could control it. She grasped its mind and held it easily.

The magekiller token burned dully in her arm—surprising her, and making the task even easier. The giant, Zhug, had once warned her that the token wouldn't help much against an experienced wizard. Such a powerful connection between Sigun and the ship, yet crude. Simple and so easily severed, like a knife through taught cloth.

Sigun's gray eyes widened. Its steady aura of power shuddered and receded. Several Terrans slumped to the floor. Shawn fell. Taunauk finished his swing and the golden warriors turned. Helesys's muscles relaxed, and she turned to face the creature.

Anger pulsed from the Sigun and the Idnauthi turned its full might against her—tried to seize her like she had seized the ship—but now its power paled in comparison. It felt like tendrils of psychic power reached out for her, but Helesys turned her remaining arcane power inward, bolstering her mind as she had bolstered her body so many times before.

Though neither alien nor weaver moved, they waged an invisible war. Sigun lashed out with a psychic maelstrom. In mindspace, it felt as if invisible tendrils, spears, and blasts were assaulting her, but Helesys dodged and slipped them all with renewed power—all while holding the ship hostage.

Even now, Helesys doubted she could face Sigun one on one in a psychic battle, but she didn't need to. She just needed to weaken him enough for her comrades to help.

Shawn, Taunauk, and the golden barbarians were nearly upon them. Sigun was trying to hold them all frozen, but the creature's psychic grip was tenuous and slipping. Sigun was only able to hold two or three of them at one time, and it alternated targets. This resulted in her comrades stuttering through their steps like a flipbook.

Shawn made it first and lunged for Sigun, but the creature floated backward. It slipped past the blades of Shawn, Taunauk, and the three glowing barbarians—freezing each of them in turn as it retreated.

Helesys went quickly to the hallway and the injured Terrans. Several were already rising and gathering the injured. Without taking her eyes off of the battle, Helesys said, "We will take you with us."

Then Helesys shouted across the frenzied room, "Hold!" And in the alien's tongue, *"Sigun, let us leave and we will spare you!"*

The battle paused, her comrades facing down Sigun, who stood wearily at the edge of the room. The Idnauthi looked down and eyed several slashes across its cloak and one across its arm. It hissed, a long and horrid sound.

"Weaver, I will give you one chance to leave. One chance to flee before the Rithdai gets you." Then Sigun slipped around the hall and Helesys heard his faint footsteps trail off into the distance.

~ ~ ~

Certain Death

"Don't go after it," Helesys called to Taunauk and Shawn.

They stood across the room, the spawning pool between her and her comrades. Taunauk's golden warriors faded, evaporating to the ether.

Shawn turned and groaned. "Remind me why we're letting the bad guy get away again?"

"Because we need to get out of here and there has to be an easier way than fighting Sigun."

"Sigun?" Shawn asked.

For a moment, Helesys forgot that her comrades hadn't understood any of her exchange with the Idnauthi. "Sigun is the creature's name."

The rogue shivered. "Gods, I hate when you speak tongues like that. It's creepy."

Taunauk backed quickly away but didn't turn from the hallway. "What did it say?"

"It said we have one chance to leave before the Rithdai attacks us."

"One of the creatures from the hallway?" Taunauk asked.

"I don't think so."

"See, that's what I mean," Shawn said. "We should've killed the bastard a moment ago."

Helesys shook her head. "I don't think we can beat Sigun. The only reason I broke free is because I took the ship from it." When her comrades looked surprised, she added, "The ship is a conduit. It was amplifying Sigun's power—it's a big dumb creature. But even now, Sigun is too powerful. It only retreated because it's never fought something that was able to fight back."

Taunauk's face grew dark. "What about the seams?"

Her wand's voice was quiet in her head. *The only seams that I sense are in the direction of Sigun, at the helm of the ship.*

Helesys shook her head. "Toward the helm. We can't take that risk—we'll have to find another way."

Beside them, one of the Terrans—a stocky human man began muttering wildly. "We need to get out of here. Out of here, I tell you. The Rithdai is coming."

One of the elder women grabbed the man by the shoulders. "What are you talking about?"

"I saw it," he muttered. "When that thing was controlling me. I saw it. It's huge! We can't—"

"We need to get out of here," someone else said.

A young elf stood stoically. Her hair was a ragged, fiery red. "There is a hatch. I saw it. It must lead to the dungeon—"

"Anywhere is better than here," someone interrupted.

Helesys looked to the young elf and smirked. "Take us there, girl. We will follow you." To Shawn, she said, "Lead with her."

A horrid groan echoed through the room. All eyes turned and found the green oval—the window to Sigun's mind and the Idnauthi's history—changed from green to orange. The same as the trap from the hallway.

Then the oval grew, stretching from the ceiling to the floor.

"Go, now!" Taunauk shouted.

Shawn and the other Terrans took off down the hall, dragging the wounded and limping with them. Helesys and Taunauk followed, glancing from their comrades to the hall.

The floor shook as something stepped through the portal. Each footfall echoed both dully and with a screech of talons. The creature bellowed—its voice a horrid mix of creatures: The shriek of an eagle, the roar of a bear, and the wet gasp of an Idnauthi.

~

The heroes and Terrans ran, Shawn and the red-haired elf leading them through twists and turns, past derelict rooms— sitting rooms with twisted chairs, rooms full of blank oval portals, empty slave rooms, and empty spawning rooms.

"By Movernus," Shawn exclaimed up ahead. "This place is massive!"

Helesys thought back to the memories she'd watched through the green portal, memories that seemed fleeting now that she had some distance from it. The Idnauthi sent a single ship to new worlds. *Only a single ship.*

She had this all wrong. These weren't merely vessels to bring hosts back to the homeworld. This ship was meant to act as a home base—meant to conquer planets.

"This is a warship," Helesys said. "And thankfully it's not full of crew."

"There are others!" one man exclaimed. "The frozen ones."

"Keep it down," Helesys replied in hushed voice as they ran. She thought back to her visions of Sigun placing the other

Idnauthi into freezing sleep. "It will take time to wake them," she added. "By then we will be long gone."

A shrill howl echoed through the corridors, and sent shivers down Helesys's back.

"How much further?" Shawn asked.

The young, red-haired elf leading them gasped, "We're nearly there."

The floor rumbled, and through the hall came the screeching and scraping of giant steps just behind them.

They ran through another salve room, full of empty pods. Taunauk stopped suddenly at the edge of the hall, turned, and growled.

"Run!" the barbarian shouted to the others. "Find the exit!"

Helesys spun around, glancing to her comrades—Shawn, who was swept along with the free Terrans, and Taunauk, who was going to buy them time. She did not want to leave either— not to whatever uncertain dangers lay further ahead in the ship nor to the certain danger fast approaching.

"Go! Get the hatch open!" Helesys said, turning around and facing the derelict room—choosing certain danger.

Helesys kept hold of the ship, of that huge, pitiful creature, and kept some power to bolster her body and mind, but she funneled her remaining power to her gauntlet. Arcane energy swelled and crackled across the metal. The weaver dredged the depths of power, then amplified it with the Gar of Shéslang until the gauntlet was rattling in her shoulder.

She waited, teeth gritted, holding a tenuous grip on so much power.

The Rithdai rounded the corner.

Whatever the creature had been was twisted into a nightmare. Its body was hulking, ten feet tall at the shoulders, the whole of it a bruised purple color. It was covered in thick, jagged plates—like bone armor—that swelled and fell like waves as it charged, barely containing the muscles beneath. It's wide feet lined with sickle-curved talons.

And all the armor seemed to converge on its head, which seemed a single, solid mass of bone as wide as a man that tapered into the vicious-looking hooked beak like that of an enormous snapping turtle or an eagle.

The Rithdai came for them, shrieking high, the claws of its feet tearing chunks from the floor.

Helesys braced herself with the spear, and fired. Purple power ripped across the room, splintering the edges of pods. The weaver held her breath as it slammed into the Rithdai—

And the blast split around its armor. Shards of power slammed into the walls behind it, blasting away chunks of wall.

The great beast stuttered in its charge—only briefly—and turned right for her.

Helesys had only moments. She reached out to seize the creature and hold it, but she felt nothing. The Rithdai was psychically reinforced, like its Idnauthi masters.

Taunauk roared and charged, glowing golden, power already smoking from his shoulders.

In those few breaths, Helesys churned power again, and willed her wand-arm to fire rapidly at the creature. Shot after shot hit the Rithdai, and each fell weakly against its bone plates.

Taunauk raised the Everfall shield and threw his shoulder and strength behind it. The Rithdai crashed into Everfall—the bone and ironwood echoing like a crack of thunder. Taunauk slid on the balls of his feet, but the Rithdai shoved past him.

Helesys channeled all her power inward, flooding her muscles and bones with otherworldly might. She gripped the spear and dodged to the left, hoping to slip behind her comrade—

The Rithdai turned and lunged for her. Helesys swung with the Gar of Shéslang. The spear struck with horrid impact and Helesys missed being bitten in half by its sharp beak, but the Rithdai swung its head and slammed into her.

Such an absentminded attack, and the impact sent Helesys careening across the room, shattering pods and thudding against the far wall. Her vision wavered and her ears rang. She gasped and her ribs stabbed with pain.

Somewhere across the room, Helesys heard echoes of impact, the growl of a barbarian, and the screech of the monster. Then the floor shook beneath her and the scraping of talons grew louder.

Helesys grabbed the spear and channeled all her power into herself and into it. She spun and tried to stand, but slipped on broken shards of pods, and fell to her back, the stabbing pain of her ribs muted by power.

The Rithdai was upon her in a breath, its massive, armored body blotting out the room. It snapped at her, and it was everything that the weaver could to stay out of its maw. She swung the Gar of Shéslang to counter, but each blow only succeeded in knocking her farther back across the room and then tumbling against the wall.

Golden warriors leapt onto the Rithdai's back. Repeating clangs of metal sounded over the fray, but nothing turned away the monster. Helesys was tossed and chased, barely able to stand before she was flung again. All the while feeling the ominous breeze with each near-miss of the beak.

Helesys called upon the Ring of Winter, muttering, "*Sgiath deighe*." She grimaced as the tendril of ice slipped from her nerves, sprung outward, and formed an icy wall in front of her.

The Rithdai recoiled from the shield but dove back at her, snapping and slashing with its claws. Each blow seemed to push back the magic shield—but moments were all Helesys needed. Just moments to stand.

Helesys kept her body bolstered, but funneled power to her gauntlet once more, this time tainted with the Ring of Winter. Icy power rippled from her metal arm. She rolled to her feet, unleashing icy blasts at the Rithdai.

No blast cracked the beast's armor, but each left an icy scar, chilling the bone plates. Over and over she fired, freezing and tainting the monster's hide.

It roared and lashed at her in spite of the cold. The wintery shield was nearly gone—the beak and claws only inches from her now. Helesys shunted power from her body to her spear, grasped it with both hands, brought it overhead, and slammed it down on the Rithdai's face.

A thundercrack echoed through the room as the Gar of Shéslang broke the skull plate.

The recoil of the blow sent Helesys into the air and overtop of the beast and overtop of the glowing barbarians. As she arched through the air, she emptied the rest of the Ring of Winter into her gauntlet's blasts—coating the monster's hide in ice.

And as she landed, Helesys funneled all her might into her body and into the spear. The Rithdai bellowed and spun round for her, but was met with four glowing barbarians and a bolstered sorceress.

The Rithdai was a blur of otherworldly beak and claw, but the heroes were a thunderstorm brought to earth. For three breaths, there was nothing but deafening chaos—steel cracked and shattered the armor plates while the Rithdai tore through two glowing barbarians.

In the end, Helesys, Taunauk, and one other barbarian stood over the Rithdai, overshadowing it. The beast screeched in fury even though it oozed green blood and could barely stand. The room around them, which until moments ago had been full of slave pods, was now pulverized and unrecognizable.

In the end, Taunauk stood tall and held out his axe—gesturing that Helesys should have the final blow. The weaver obliged, the crunch of her spear nearly splitting the beast's head in two. She sighed, trying to control her breathing.

Helesys would not muse on the ease with which violence came to her—would not dwell on it nor apologize for it. It was a part of her—and it would see her through the dungeon. She would make peace with it on the other side.

Beside her, the one glowing warrior faded, and Taunauk returned to normal. "We should go," he said, eyes drifting from the creature and to her. "Good fight," he added, almost as an afterthought.

Helesys would've smirked at the compliment, but her mouth fell open in muted horror—

She could no longer feel the ship. Somewhere in the fray, Helesys had lost her hold over it, or Sigun had plucked it from her grasp. Either way, it was gone and once again bolstering the blasted Idnauthi.

Worse, Helesys could feel what Sigun was doing. It was manipulating the ship—ceasing the sleep functions. She could already feel the temperature dropping in the freezing pods.

"We need to go," she said suddenly. "Sigun took the ship from me. It's waking the others."

And they would have no chance if Sigun found them before they could escape.

~

Helesys and Taunauk sprinted through the corridors. This time, the subtle direction from her wand led them to Shawn and the other survivors. Their frantic journey through the halls had led to a hangar. Easily the largest room on the ship, thick ribs lined the walls and wrapped around to a spine that ran down the center. At the end was a hatch or a *mouth*, the seam stretching nearly the width of the room.

Shawn and the others were gathered around the mouth, running hands along the seam. The rogue was trying to pry the seam open with daggers.

Shawn whipped around at the sound of their footsteps with a frenzied look in his eye that quickly faded. "Well, thank Movernus for that. I'm not sure what kind of hatch I expected, but at least it's not a sphincter."

Ignoring his comment, the weaver and barbarian ran over to the group and started searching the hatch. Taunauk grasped the lip of the hatch and tried to pull it open, but the hatch didn't budge. Even pulling together, all the escapees couldn't open it.

Helesys grunted in frustration. They didn't have time to waste.

"Taunauk," she said, causing him to pause. "See if it responds to more forceful measures." Helesys pressed her metal hand to the hatch of the ship and said, *"Protegentibus lucem."*

Her gauntlet flared with warding light, but it was the side effect that Helesys was after. In moments, her gauntlet burned scalding hot and scalding the flesh of the living ship.

Beside her, Taunauk slammed his battleaxe into the dense flesh. It cut shallow, but it cut nonetheless. Green blood oozed from each wound as Taunauk hacked into it.

Helesys flared her power, causing the light to grow blinding and the metal of her arm to grow so hot she had to kindle strength not to scream.

She reached into the mind of the ship once more—

The ship was in pain, in borderline agony, but Sigun was in control of it, commanding the ship to keep its hull closed.

"So much for that," Helesys mumbled as she let her warding light fade. She removed her metal hand, revealing a vicious, charred and cracked print in its place.

Behind them, the freed Terrans mulled about. Some held each other close while others whispered prayers.

Shawn was looking between his allies and the door. He caught the weaver's eye as she turned. "Feeling a little useless right now."

"Just keep an eye on the door. Taunauk, everyone, move out of the way."

Taunauk turned suddenly, took her meaning, and then moved the others away from her.

Helesys walked over to the bloody gashes in the wall, her wand-arm dredging power. Power churned and compounded between her wand and the Gar of Shéslang until metal rattled in her shoulder. Then the weaver bolstered her strength enough to stand the recoil.

She braced herself and leveled her gauntlet for a point-blank shot, then released.

Arcane power exploded from her hand, tearing through the flesh and bone hull of the living ship.

Helesys skidded backward on her feet before hitting something. She looked back to find that Taunauk had caught her. The two comrades nodded to one another before waving the others forward.

In front of them lay a sizzling hole four feet wide and two feet deep. Through the hole, they could see both the night sky and the shingles of the castle roof. The smell of burning flesh from the ship was overpowering, but it didn't stop any of them.

The young elf with fiery red hair volunteered to climb through first. "It's a short drop to the roof," she called once she was through. "Quickly, everyone!"

One by one, the others climbed through. Helesys, Taunauk, and Shawn waited to go through last.

The weaver turned her attention back to the ship. More Idnauthi were waking from freezing sleep—five more. Far too many for them to fight, but a few moments from now they would be long gone.

But Sigun was no longer in the control room—he was coming toward them! Helesys could feel him flying through the halls.

Helesys turned, calling once more on her artifacts and on the Ring of Winter. She let loose repeated shots toward the entrance, each slamming into the walls and coalescing with ice. In moments, the entrance was walled off. She imagined it wouldn't hold the Idnauthi for long.

Just a few moments more was all they needed.

The others had climbed through. Shawn was next and through in a breath. Taunauk shimmied through a moment later. Then Helesys climbed through.

And as she slipped through, she heard the crunching of ice and the alien scream of Sigun.

Helesys dropped to the roof of the castle—only for a moment considering the height, the slope, and the utter lack of walkways around them. The group clung perilously to the slope. Her thoughts turned briefly to the jade lemur statuette, but there was no way they could all fit on its back.

Above them, the Idnauthi ship loomed. From inside, the true size of the ship had been impossible to guess, but the side of the ship stretched to the edge of her vision, so long that it appeared to be another part of the castle. The skin of it was slick with scales and from the edges, Helesys could see silhouettes of hundreds of spindly tentacles waving in the still air— it looked as if the night sky was alive.

It looked as if some time ago the Idnauthi ship had crashed into the roof of the castle and embedded itself.

She lay flat on the incline, then reached once more for the ship. Sigun still had a monstrous grasp upon it. There was no way he would fall for the same trick again.

Luckily, Helesys had another. This time she reached for the engines—the one part of the ship that relied on magic, the one connection that she could see blazing bright in mindspace. She grasped the engines and activated them.

The ship and the roof of the dungeon began to shake, and above them, the ship rumbled to life.

Hot air whipped across the rooftop. Behind her, Helesys heard screams as the others held tight to the shingles.

Helesys, look! her wand said.

A short distance up the roof was an opening. It lay between the crushed section of roof and the hull. An escape back into the castle and whatever room lay beneath the ship.

It will be safer there, the wand added.

Helesys called back to her comrades and pointed up to the opening. "We must go there!" Then she, Taunauk, and Shawn helped the others climb into the opening.

It wasn't until Helesys was in the crevice and to the space beyond that she fully engaged the living ship's engines. A thunderclap sounded around them as the ship vanished up into the sky. Wind roared past them, but they felt no heat.

Helesys looked up through the expanse of broken roof and watched the shrinking fire of the ship with satisfaction. The ship had destroyed such a large swathe of the roof that, for a moment, the night sky was all she saw. The elf held a sliver of peace before her hearing came back to her.

As the wind died down, the smell returned: The dry tinge of decay and ammonia.

It wasn't until she looked down at the sprawling room—an immense attic with rib-like joists above—that she saw the true nature of their plight. They stood on a great pile of bodies that cascaded down some hundred feet. More lay all throughout the sprawling room, packed so tightly that she hadn't realized that she was standing on the mummified back of a Terran.

Only then did she hear the muffled screams and whimpers of the other freed Terrans, huddling together and glancing around at the horror.

~ ~ ~

The Attic

"There must be another room. There must be another room!" one of the men muttered.

The light from the stars shone bright through the giant hole in the castle roof, illuminating the grisly scene. Densely packed bodies stretched out across the attic and disappeared into the gloom.

Helesys called on her warding light and her gauntlet glowed bright as day. She held it overhead and gasped at the sight.

From atop their mound of the mummified dead, she saw the true scale of the attic and the castle. The Idnauthi ship had seemed immense, but the gaping hole it left was dwarfed by the castle—by the dungeon. The mound of the dead sloped down and down. Her light had pushed away the darkness for hundreds of feet—but even this was just the ends of the slope of the dead. At the bottom, the attic trusses hung one hundred feet overhead. Vertical beams as thick as trees rose through the bodies and to the distant ceiling.

And still the attic stretched on in all directions, reminding Helesys of the sprawling greenhouse from below the wizard Amadeus's study—an utterly immense indoor space.

Shawn leaned in to her and Taunauk, and whispered, "You know, we could still go back. Find another spot on the roof to blast through."

Taunauk grunted uneasily, squeezing the grips of his axe. "I don't think we'll be that lucky. Do you see the slope up there? It's nearly flat."

Helesys said, "Taunauk's right. We'd just come through somewhere else in this place. Somewhere without a hill to land on."

Shawn sighed. "*Stercus.* Well, at least all the bodies are—"

At the bottom of the mound, at the farthest reaches of Helesys's light, there was movement. A Terran stood at the edge of her vision and shuffled backward into the shadows.

"Did you see that?" Shawn asked.

"Yes," she replied.

"Whatever gods that be," Shawn muttered, "I kindly ask that we go back to fighting dragons and fishmen and lizards and—"

Shawn paused just as three more Terran shapes shuffled back into the darkness.

"Shit," he muttered.

~

Helesys and Taunauk led them down the mummified slope, while Shawn stayed at their back. The group of surviving Terran slaves huddled together in the middle. When they had made it down to the bottom, they kept going across flats of the dead.

All the while, other Terrans watched idly from the outskirts of her light. Most slipped in and out of view, but some stood still and watched their procession like statues.

Blank-faced statues.

"What are they?" one of their group whispered.

"Shh! Don't speak of them," said another.

Shawn added, "They are nothing we wish to know."

Helesys reached out twice, stretching her wand and her mind like she did in the to see if she could reach the creatures, but both times she felt nothing—absolutely nothing.

Whatever they were was alright with Helesys, so long as they stayed at the edge of her light.

Meanwhile, the weaver followed her wand. The faintest pull of direction, leading them across the attic.

What do you sense? Helesys asked her wand. *Are you still there?*

I am with you, always. It is possibly another seam, but I don't know for certain.

I thought you had vanished, the weaver said. *That you were just a trick of my mind.*

I speak when needed. It is more efficient to communicate through feeling.

Did you always speak to me this way? she asked. *Before we were trapped in the dungeon?*

I don't remember anymore than you do. I remember blastshells and warfare, dancing at balls—all the same things that you remember.

Helesys said internally, *One-Mind said that the connection it repaired between us happened before we came to the dungeon. Do you remember what was severed or why?*

I feel that it was a connection between us. One to prevent us from speaking as we do now. That is puzzling… If we were joined to repair a limb or for warfare, then we should've been fully connected. Otherwise, we would not be fully operational.

It could be sabotage.

That is possible.

What about cutting my hair? Helesys asked. *Do you remember that?*

...No. I do not.

What about my sister, Aradi? Or my mother, Wynbella?

Your sister, yes. I did not like her, but I don't remember the reason.

Neither do I, but those memories escape me—

"Helesys."

The weaver glanced to Taunauk. Though he walked with axe and Everfall in hand, he was eyeing her curiously.

"Are you sure you're alright?" he asked. "You look far away."

For the briefest moment, Helesys considered not telling her comrade about her wand speaking to her, if only so she could sort it out completely. But she pushed the reservation aside. Taunauk was her brother-at-arms.

"Since One-Mind repaired the connection in my gauntlet, my wand has been speaking to me."

The barbarian's eyebrows raised.

From behind the group, Shawn whispered loudly, "Wait, what? Your wand is talking to you?"

Helesys sighed, and Taunauk continued staring.

"Yes," Helesys said. "It's difficult to explain."

Shawn asked, "What does she sound like?"

"She?" Helesys replied. "It's a wand. It sounds like a wand."

"Oh," the rogue said dejectedly. "I just assumed because my coin definitely sounded like a man."

"You have a talking coin?" one of the Terrans asked quietly.

"Yeah. I think it leads to drink. Or it's supposed to. It steered me wrong once before. Come to think of it, I don't know if it's been correct yet..."

Shawn is strange, her wand said.

Indeed, Helesys replied internally.

"Does it speak?" Taunauk asked beside her.

"Yes, though it was silent for most of our escape. It has always spoken to me, in a way. All the sense of direction and guidance has been from the wand, but felt intrinsically, as if it were no different from a gut feeling."

Taunauk grunted in acknowledgement as he looked across the attic. "I ask because the spirits speak to me as well."

It was Helesys's turn to look surprised. "What do they say?"

"Little. And I have asked them many questions. I asked why they are attached to me, and what trapped us here. They have no recollection of the time before—in that, we are the same."

"Well, what *do* they say?" she asked.

Taunauk sighed wearily. "They tell me to journey to the Godpeak and to speak with the spirits there. They say that it is not their place to answer my questions."

Helesys put her elven hand on her friend's shoulder. "Then we will get to the Godpeak and find the truth, either way."

From behind the group, Shawn said, "Isn't that just the way? You think you're close to getting answers and they just pull the rug right out from under you."

~

Conversation ebbed between the heroes, while the freed Terrans began to whisper amongst themselves. They talked of lives past and of wandering the dungeon. For some, being trapped by the Idnauthi was the only peace they had known.

All the while, they walked deeper and deeper into the attic, and the blank-faced Terrans mulled around the edges of Helesys's light. If the weaver could've blared her light any brighter then she would've, but she wouldn't risk using up too much of her power—not when the creatures were so easily kept at bay and not when they had so much further left to go.

A scream echoed through the attic, so faint at first that Helesys questioned whether she had heard anything at all.

Helesys turned, scanning the outskirts of the blazing light from her gauntlet, but she saw nothing save for a half dozen Terrans staring back at her.

"What is it, Helesys?" Taunauk asked.

The entire group stopped and parted so that Helesys could look around them.

"You don't hear that?" she asked.

The scream grew louder still—

Until Helesys finally recognized the wet, raspy voice of an Idnauthi.

She spun around, looking back the way they came to the distant hole in the attic where the Idnauthi ship had rocketed off into the sky. In the distance, a tiny form was growing—sprinting toward them.

"You dithtt! You insolent carapaci! Hidh tii!" Sigun's screams devolved into obscenities as the alien raced toward them, cape billowing.

Helesys shoved the freed slaves out of the way. Then leveled her arm and churned what power she could without losing her warding light. Then she let arcane power soar across the attic. The purple blasts from her wand almost seemed to blot out the light as they flew.

Sigun twisted and turned in the air as it flew, narrowly dodging the blasts; one ripped the cloak from its back.

"You'll pay for that, dithtt!"

Then the alien was upon them and its terrible form shone brilliantly in the warding light. Whatever majesty and composure the Idnauthi had aboard the ship was gone. Sigun's purple skin was marred, the tendrils shorn off, and oozing blue blood.

Taunauk stepped forward to meet the beast. Glowing warriors materialized beside him, bearing swords and axes. They lunged and swung, but moved in stutter-steps as Sigun assaulted their minds.

Helesys felt the alien touch of Sigun reach for her, but the weaver turned power inward and bolstered her mind. She stepped backward reflexively and slipped the creature's psychic tendrils—

But back on the ship, Helesys had turned her full power to defense. Here, she could not risk doing the same—not without losing her light. Neither the Gar of Shéslang nor the Ring of Winter could not bolster her psychic resolve.

Already, the warding light was receding. Where before it had stretched out for hundreds of feet—now it might have only been one hundred. She dared not turn away from Sigun, but she could see from the corner of her vision that the attic had grown small in the gloom.

And with it, the blank-faced Terrans approached.

Sigun slipped the stuttering and spasmodic swings of Taunauk and the glowing barbarians, even passed Shawn—the rogue was hanging with his feet off the ground, his outline faint and flickering, as if he might disappear into thin air. And Helesys stepped back, past the freed slaves who were cowering in the same stuttering motion as the barbarians—

In Sigun's reckless anger, he was psychically assaulting them all.

Sigun slipped them all, then grasped the first freed Terran he came to: An older human, with wide bloodshot eyes. Sigun grasped his neck with one spindly hand, then twisted. Horrid cracks echoed through the attic and the man hung limply in the air—not dropping to the ground for several seconds as Sigun held him psychically.

"*No more carapaci*," Sigun hissed, as he grabbed the next— the young elf with red hair. His long fingers wrapped nearly all the way around her neck and shoulder.

"No!" Helesys screamed, raising her arm and funneling power to her blast.

Sigun turned, staring at her with milky gray eyes. All at once, Helesys felt stabbing pain in her skull as dozens of psychic lashes were turned against her. Her knees buckled and her readied blast soared high across the room.

She would've collapsed to her knees, but Sigun held her fast. She opened her watery eyes and saw her comrades turned toward her—frozen. In the shock of the moment, Sigun had overpowered her and then regained its hold on the others.

Her warding light was faint, barely illuminating her comrades. Her grasp on the spell was tenuous, as if she were holding onto a ledge by her fingertips. Somehow, the prideful bastard let her keep the light.

Behind Taunauk and the glowing barbarians' motionless faces, Helesys saw others—

The blank-faced Terrans surrounded them by the hundreds, barely twenty feet away. Their eyes white, their faces smudged into blurry approximations. Even the clothes on their bodies were blurred so that the lines between skin and clothes were indistinguishable.

Sigun floated closer, holding the paralyzed elf girl. She stared at Helesys, eyes wide with terror.

"*Look at me, weaver. You might've escaped, but that hole you made in our ship sucked me through when you shot it into space. I nearly missed the roof when I fell. Lucky for me. Not so lucky for you, dithtt. Do you know what you are to me now?*

"Nothing more than hiis—meat."

Sigun's face tendrils flared out and something underneath chattered. It lifted the little girl's head up to its tendrils. And Helesys had the horrible vision of a beaked mouth ready to open up.

Helesys felt like time had stopped. Though her body was frozen, she still had the smallest grasp of magic. She might lose the light but she would not die to Sigun, nor allow anymore to perish by him.

She reached out for her comrades—for Taunauk and Shawn—and found that Sigun's grasp was most slippery on the rogue. Whatever was causing Shawn to flicker was *his* doing and not Sigun's. So Helesys bolstered Shawn—her scant power was magnified by the Gar of Shéslang and the rogue vanished—

Completely vanished.

Sigun stopped and turned, sensing that one of its quarry had slipped from its grasp.

The light went out.

Slashes sounded. An Idnauthi screamed. And then everyone screamed—as Sigun's psychic grasp disappeared. Helesys kept bolstering Shawn's power, but turned the rest toward her warding light.

Light washed over the attic—just enough to illuminate the group.

The blank-faced Terrans were a sea around them.

Taunauk and the barbarians stood strong again, facing outward. The freed Terrans crouched in the middle, holding tight to the red-haired elf. Shawn stood facing Sigun—the alien was gravely wounded, dripping blue blood from dozens of cuts and doubled over, clutching a deep wound across its stomach.

The rogue stood defiantly, a blue blade in one hand and a black blade in the other. The whole of him—clothes, hair, even his daggers—seemed to radiate mist or fog, as if the rogue was dissolving into dust.

Sigun glared at them, its gray eyes narrowed at Shawn. *"You.. You… What in the stars are you?"*

Sigun's voice was raspy as it stepped haggardly backward… closer and closer to the waiting blank-faced Terrans.

"It's like you're not there. Like I can't grasp you or remember you. Like you're a—"

The blank-faced mob grasped the Idnauthi. Sigun's eyes went wide and then white as it was pulled deep into the crowd. In seconds, there wasn't even a hole in the crowd to mark where Sigun disappeared.

"Funny," Shawn said, relaxing his arms, misty glow fading. "That's how I feel about me, too."

Helesys relaxed her power—all except the light—and shuddered, for she could no longer sense Sigun at all. The Idnauthi was already gone, as if his mind had been dissolved in a sea of emptiness.

Helesys breathed deep, then flared her warding light, pushing away the crowd of absent faces. They backed away without flinching or uttering a sound, lingering in the harsh shadows cast by those of Helesys's group.

Moments later, the red-haired girl was hugging Helesys tightly across the waist, breath quivering against her. The weaver stroked her hair with her elven hand while her gauntlet blazed bright. She felt so small to Helesys, and the weaver's heart went out to her.

Soon the other freed Terrans stood and leaned close, holding the girl and Helesys. Taunauk's glowing warriors faded, leaving behind only him. Both he and Shawn leaned in as well, wrapping their arms around the group.

Helesys knew herself to be few things in her past life, one of which was a soldier. It was so easy to turn to violence that she often thought she was made for it. *To task*, Taunauk had often reminded them—the task of escape. This had been easy too, to set her mind to nothing else except the path in front of her. She'd given little thought to what she had been in the life before, and far less thought to how far they had come through the dungeon… and how much further they had left to go.

But in that moment, huddled with her comrades and found family, she thought of nothing at all. She merely relished in their warm embrace.

The weaver held her metal hand above the huddled group so that the light would shine brightly. A beacon of hope against the maddening world.

~ ~ ~

NEXT TIME ON
*A BATTLEAXE AND
A METAL ARM*
Book 11:

*The Laboratory of
Mr. Mask*
Available February 2022

Spoiler–Free excerpt from *BAMA 11*

Helesys had burned the warding light since they set foot in the attic and would continue to burn it because it was the only thing that kept the creatures at bay.

She'd been afraid to sleep at first, afraid that she would lose the spell, that in the moments it would take to wake her the creatures would close in around them and carry off one of her comrades or one of the freed Terrans that depended on them. Turn them into one more of the blank faces that lurked at the edge of the light.

She'd been afraid to risk sleep because she had seen the creatures carry away one of the Idnauthi. Sigun—the alien that had fallen from the ship—came for them in the attic. Nearly bested Helesys, Taunauk, and Shawn at the same time. Even with all that power, when the light fell, the blank-faced Terrans carried Sigun off into the darkness and the poor bastard couldn't even scream.

Sometimes at the edge of the light, Helesys would see the smudged form of the alien lurking with the other creatures. The powerful visage of the alien reduced to a child's painting—mute and smudged—and all the more terrifying for what it symbolized.

Half a dozen lives ago, the giant, Zhug, had said that there were gods trapped here in the dungeon, and that there were things that even the gods feared. He warned the heroes of the many lingering deaths that awaited them. Helesys had believed his words, but she hadn't understood. Now she did.

No—Helesys wouldn't allow such a fate to befall them. Not to those that trusted her or those that depended on her.

To be continued February 2022

Thank you for Reading

I hope you enjoyed reading this story as much as I enjoyed writing it.

If you did, I would massively appreciate a short review on Amazon or your favorite book website. Reviews are crucial for any author, and a starred review or even just a line or two can make a huge difference.

It's especially true for the start of a series. Thanks and I hope you enjoy the next one!

Looking for more Engrossing Fantasy?

You might like **Tales from Another World,** an ongoing short story series containing stories about sorcerers, druids, mortals, gods, thieves, and all other manner of Terrans.

The 2nd and 3rd installments are out and they may or may not have ties to the world of *A Battleaxe and a Metal Arm*. So, if you're looking for more engrossing fantasy stories, read on and see how deep the rabbit hole goes.

What questions do you have about *A Battleaxe and a Metal Arm*?

If you've read this far, hopefully you'll read a bit further—both in this book and across the series. I'm not sure how most authors write serials and how much of it is flying by the seat of their pants, but that's not how I do things. For all the major questions that might come up in BAMA, I already have answers for 95% of them. Same goes for the major plot points, twists and climaxes. That might sound boring to some, especially some of you other authors who enjoy variations of writing into the dark, but I think having a solid blueprint is paramount to writing a long series.

So, what questions do you have about the story? Here are a few:

1) ~~What is the dungeon?~~ It's a soul trap of overwhelming size and power. But where did it come from? Is it a force of nature or an ill-made weapon, or perhaps something else entirely? In the real world it looks like a giant cloud with faces writhing just beneath the surface. Helesys speculates that the

reason no one remembers it is because it's so horrific their minds blot it out!

2) Who were Helesys and Taunauk before they got trapped? We've learned that Helesys was both a soldier and might have been elven royalty. Taunauk was an outlander either outcast or sent on some kind of a quest. How well did they know each other beforehand?

3) How did Helesys get her metal arm? Likely through injury, amputation, and replacement.

4) Who is Shawn? Why does he feel so familiar to Helesys and Taunauk? The group speculates that they were traveling together for unknown reasons.

5) Who is the Wolf King and what sinister plans does he have for our heroes? How did he come to rule over the Dungeon? How does the Gatekeeper factor into all this?

6) Who is the mysterious voice encountered on the white sandy shores of Meridian? Why do they seek the death of the Wolf-King? ...And why did they choose the heroes?

Did I miss any questions? Probably. Connect with me and other *BAMA* fans on social media and compare questions!

I've got plans. I've got answers. And I've got them on a drip-feed. Keep reading and expect to find out a little more to the mysteries with each installment. Hopefully, you're as excited about this series as I am.

Connect with the Author

If you want to stay up to date on the latest about Samuel's publishing news and blog, check out his website and consider signing up for his monthly newsletter.

www.SamuelFlemingBooks.com

Samuel can also be found on Reddit, Goodreads and Facebook.

Samuel Fleming is a Science Fiction and Fantasy author.

He grew up in Maryland, spending most of his time swimming and writing. Swimming gave him a lot of time to daydream, so the two hobbies complemented each other well. Idle day dreams turned into stories, some of which stuck with him for years. These days he swims a little less and writes a lot more.

He loves a good story no matter the medium: Books, TV, video games, comics, tabletop RPG's, or podcasts–most of which he attempts to share with his wife and three kids, and occasionally on his blog.

9 781954 679290